PASTA FACTORY

HANA MACHOTKA

HOUGHTON MIFFLIN COMPANY

Boston · 1992

ACKNOWLEDGMENTS

Many thanks to Ed Marritz, who helped conceive the idea for this book and was essential in its execution. Special thanks to Fortunato and Jerry Di Natale for welcoming me into their factory and contributing their time and expertise. To Anna Bilotta, Jean-Claude Pierre, and the entire staff of Tutta Pasta, who were always very friendly and helpful. To Kay Haran for being there. To Leda Marritz, Alessia Cook, Selina Morales, Fiona Luhrmann, Malik Williams, Karen Halperin, and Rachel Shane for their unbounding enthusiasm. To my editor, Matilda Welter, for her confidence and encouragement, to Carol Goldenberg, for her fine design. And to my agent, Laura Blake, for her dedicated efforts on my behalf.

Library of Congress Cataloging-in-Publication Data

Machotka, Hana.
    Pasta factory / Hana Machotka.
        p.   cm.
    Summary: Depicts a trip to the Tutta Pasta factory in New York City.
    ISBN 0-395-60197-5
    1. Tutta Pasta Corp. — Juvenile literature.   2. Pasta factories — New York (N.Y.) — Juvenile literature.   3. n-us-ny.   [1. Tutta Pasta Corp.   2. Pasta factories.]   I. Title.
TP435.M3M23   1992   92-4333
664'.755 — dc20   CIP
                            AC

HOR 10 9 8 7 6 5 4 3 2 1

For David Wolkenberg,

an exceptional teacher and friend,
without whom this book would never have been written.

Pasta, which is the Italian word for paste or dough, may have originated in China thousands of years ago, although no one knows for sure. What is sure is that pasta has been a favorite food of people around the world for a very long time, and different regions have developed their own special ways of preparing it.

Pasta is tasty, economical, nutritious, and always fun to eat. You can change its flavor by adding any one of hundreds of sauces. You can make yourself silly trying to get it from the plate to your mouth. And you can choose from a variety of shapes: squiggles, ribbons, threads, ropes, elbows, rice grains, stars, bow ties, butterflies, wheels, flowers, and rings.

Have you ever wondered who makes pasta and how?

Fortunato Di Natale is the owner of the Tutta Pasta factory. He brought his recipes from Italy when he came to America as a young man. Now he sells so much pasta that he has expanded his factory to a large space in New Jersey.

Children curious to see how noodles are made at Tutta Pasta must wear paper hats to keep hair from getting into the food. Fortunato's son Jerry shows visitors around the factory.

"Tutta Pasta is Italian for 'all pasta,'" he explains. "All you need to make pasta is flour, eggs, and water. The flour we use is called durum semolina. It's a high-quality flour that's easy to roll out."

Jerry takes the visitors to a room with an enormous silo. "This holds the flour until we're ready to use it," he continues. "When we need flour, we push a button on this panel. The flour shoots from the silo through pipes along the ceiling to the mixing machine. Another pipe brings in an egg and water mixture. We use only egg whites because so many people want to avoid the cholesterol in egg yolks," he explains.

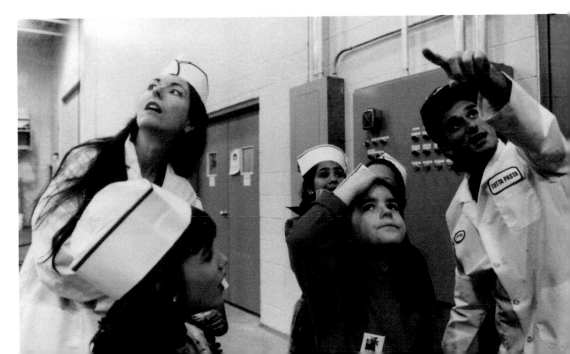

The next stop is a machine called a laminator. Here the dough is pressed into sheets by cylinders that work very much like rolling pins.

A worker lifts a big bag of flour and empties it into

a bin. Next he adds a container of eggs and milk and pushes a button which starts the blades rotating, mixing the flour up into a lumpy mass. With the press of another button, the bin empties its contents into the laminator.

The machine whirs and hums and soon a sheet of dough appears below. It winds up onto a spindle to form a large roll.

Jerry brings some scraps of dough for the children to feel. Usually scraps like this get recycled back into the laminator.

When enough dough has been made, a worker opens up the machine and scrapes off the leftover dough with a knife. Then he washes the machine thoroughly. Everyone works very hard to maintain the highest degree of cleanliness at the factory.

Now the roll of dough is pressed into an even thinner sheet that travels through a steamer. The steamer heats the dough up to 220 degrees Fahrenheit for five minutes to kill any bacteria. This process is called pasteurization.

As the dough comes out, it is cut into ribbons by rotating blades. Depending on the width of the cut, the noodle will be fettuccine (little ribbons), linguine (little tongues), spaghetti (little strings), or capellini (angel hair).

A worker folds each batch into plastic containers. As the containers move along a conveyor belt, a plastic sheet covers each box, which is then sealed with a hot press. At the same time, a small tube sucks air out of the boxes as a mixture of carbon dioxide and nitrogen replaces it. This mixture prolongs the shelf life of fresh pasta from a few days to six weeks. Finally, another worker attaches stickers that list important information: the type of noodle, the factory where it was made, the ingredients, cooking instructions, and an expiration date.

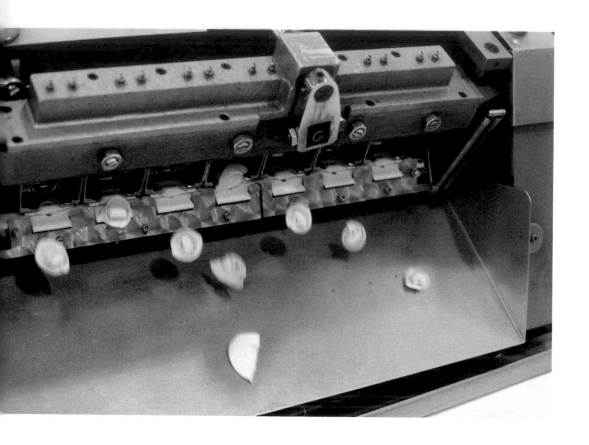

"Click-flap, click-flap, click-flap" is the sound coming from a tortellini machine as small tortellini drop into a tray. "This machine makes five hundred tortellini per minute," Jerry explains. One worker puts on a new roll of dough. Another worker fills a bucket with cheese filling. Jerry explains how this machine cuts small circles from the dough. Cheese filling drops onto each circle, which is folded over. Then the two ends are bent around to form a ring just before the finished tortellini pops out.

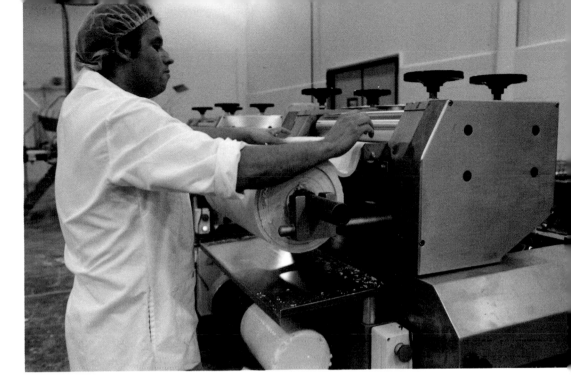

Scraps of leftover dough from the tortellini machine drop onto a conveyor belt and collect in a bucket. They will be returned to the laminator to be pressed into a new roll.

Nearby, a machine makes red tortelloni. Tortelloni are a little bit larger than tortellini and they are red because tomatoes have been added to the dough. Another machine is making green tortelloni which has had spinach added to the dough. The two batches will be mixed with white tortelloni to make tricolored noodles.

A conveyor belt takes the tortelloni to a white steam box, where it is first steamed and then quickly cooled to prevent the growth of bacteria.

The tortelloni are ready to be boxed. From the conveyor belt they drop into clear plastic boxes. Small copper weights in the weighing machine help to make sure that the right amount of noodles is in each package. Again the boxes are sealed with plastic and the nitrogen–carbon dioxide mix ture replaces the air in the box. Labels are attached and the boxes are stored in large cardboard cartons. A forklift transfers them to the refrigerator, where they will wait to be shipped out.

Driftwood Library
of Lincoln City
801 S.W. Highway 101, #201
Lincoln City, Oregon 97367

Some noodles are made in an extruder, which presses dough through forms called dies to give them special shapes. Squiggly openings create a spiral-shaped noodle called fusilli (spindles). Other dies create shapes like conchiglietti (shells), vermicelli (little worms), ziti (tubes), rigatoni (elbows), stellini (little stars), and rotelle (wheels).

Some people like to buy dry pasta. It keeps a long time because it has been processed in a drying tank. The pasta is loaded through the little doors at the end. Hot air blows over it for twenty-four hours until it is hard and dry.

Overhead pipes propel the dry pasta down a spiral chute into large storage bins, where it is stored until ready for packaging in cellophane bags.

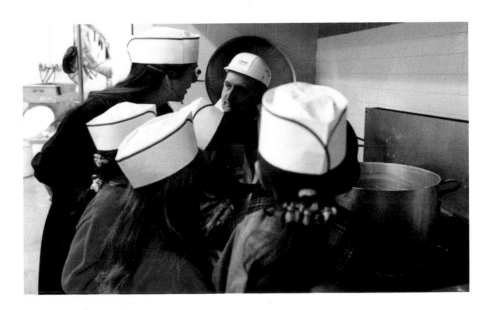

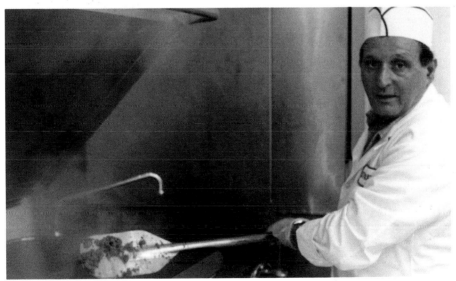

Delicious aromas welcome visitors to the kitchen. Here Fortunato points out several sauces cooking on the stove. He stirs a large vat of ground meat that will go into making a meat sauce.

Fortunato explains that the tomatoes in the sauce are the best tomatoes imported from Italy, and the onions, parsley and spices are always fresh. Fortunato ladles out some finished sauce for everyone to taste.

It's deliciously tart and hot! And no wonder; Fortunato takes no short cuts in making the product, Jerry explains.

Large blocks of romano cheese are waiting to be grated to make filling for tortellini. Jerry cuts off a sample to taste. Then he explains how the grating machine works.

The next stop is the storage room. Here are tall stacks of boxes, plastic containers for sauce, cans of tomato paste, whole tomatoes and olive oil from Italy, black olives, garlic, salt, and bread crumbs.

A curtain of plastic strips keeps the cool air inside the enormous refrigerator. Stored here are boxes of cheese, spinach, basil, and fresh pasta waiting to be shipped out. A worker on a forklift gives the children a ride.

Next door is a tool shop, where the machinist can repair broken-down machines. There are tools, nuts, bolts, and machine parts everywhere.

Tutta Pasta has its own laboratory. Every day samples from each batch are tested. One machine tests the moisture content in a box of noodles. Dry pasta should have no more than 10 to 20 percent moisture. Another machine tests oxygen content. Too much would spoil the food. In addition, a sample of each batch of food is sent to a laboratory that checks for salmonella and other bacteria.

Behind the factory is a loading dock, where a truck is
waiting to be filled with cartons of pasta.

When the tour is over, Jerry gives out samples of
tomato sauce and pasta. The children can hardly wait
to try it.

The next time you are eating pasta, you will know how it was made. But did you know you can also make pasta at home? Making it can be almost as much fun as eating it!

Please pass the pasta!